gigi

This book belongs to:

Princess _____

gigi
God's Little Princess

By Sheila Walsh

Illustrated by Meredith Johnson

www.tommynelson.com

A Division of Thomas Nelson, Inc.
www.ThomasNelson.com

Scripture taken from the International Children's Bible® , New Century Version® . Copyright © 1986, 1988, 1999 by Tommy Nelson® , a Division of Thomas Nelson, Inc. Used by permission.

Published in Nashville, Tennessee, by Tommy Nelson®, a Division of Thomas Nelson, Inc.

Tommy Nelson books may be purchased in bulk for educational, business, fundraising, or sales promotional use. For information, please e-mail SpecialMarkets@ThomasNelson.com.

Library of Congress Cataloging-in-Publication Data

Walsh, Sheila.
  Gigi : God's little princess / by Sheila Walsh ; illustrations by Meredith Johnson.
      p. cm.
  Summary: Gigi, who has always known she is a princess, is confused at first by her parents' explanation of what makes her royal.
  ISBN 1-4003-0529-2 (jacketed hardcover)
  ISBN 1-4003-0741-4 (hardcover)
  [1. Christian life—Fiction. 2. Princesses—Fiction. 3. Family life—Fiction.] I. Johnson, Meredith, ill. II. Title.
  PZ7.W16894Gi 2005
  [E]—dc22

2005001774

Printed in the United States of America
05 06 07 08 PHX 6 5 4 3 2

This book
is dedicated
to all God's
little princesses.

Gigi was a princess. She had known it from birth.

Every night when her daddy kissed her forehead, he would say, "Goodnight, princess. Sweet dreams!"

At times Gigi wondered why they didn't live in a castle and where *were* the royal jewels?

She assumed they were locked away in a vault somewhere for safekeeping, and when she was all grown up or ten—whichever came first—they would be presented to her.

One thing troubled Gigi. She didn't exactly look like a traditional princess.

No matter how hard she scrubbed, she could not get rid of the freckles on her nose.

No matter how hard she brushed her hair, she could not get it to lie down and behave.

"I *so* need a crown to flatten this," she thought.

Gigi's best friend was Frances. Frances was not royal, but Gigi loved her anyway.

"One must bond with one's subjects," she told Frances.

"Thank you, Your Highness," Frances replied
with appropriate gratitude.

Gigi loved to discover things. She assumed that her royal ancestors had left treasures for her, and she was determined to find each one.

So far she had uncovered four buttons, two pieces of velvet ribbon, and a jar that may once have been a glass slipper. Her future looked promising.

Gigi was sure that one day she would rule over many subjects who would bow when she entered a room.

She practiced on her cat.

The cat seemed reluctant to cooperate.

"This attitude must change if you expect to be great in my kingdom," she told Lord Fluffy.

Her favorite thing to do was to have a tea party in the backyard (or the "outer court," as she called it) with Frances.

"May I ask a question, Your Royal Highness?" Frances asked one day.

"Speak," Gigi replied.

"What makes you a princess, and why am I not a princess?"

"Isn't it obvious?" Gigi asked.

"Not immediately," Frances replied.

"Hmm," said Gigi.

That night Gigi asked her father, "Daddy, what makes me a princess?"

"You have always been a princess," he said.

"Yes, but where are the royal jewels and where is my crown and when do I begin my reign?" she asked. "I think I'm ready."

Her father laughed. "I think you are ready to go to sleep, young lady. Goodnight, princess. Sweet dreams."

The next morning, Gigi decided to clear up the matter with her mom.

"Mommy, Frances asked me what makes me a princess and why is she not a princess."

"You are both princesses," her mom replied.

Gigi was shocked by this revelation!

She sat on her bed with Lord Fluffy.

"Should I be the one to tell Frances?
Will I have to share my jewels?
Will she have her own jewels?
How will the land be divided?
To whom will Lord Fluffy bow first?"

"May I please call Frances?" she asked her mom.

"Yes, you may. You can use the kitchen phone if you like."

"This is royal business, Mom. I will need to use the pink phone," Gigi replied.

"Frances, are you sitting down?" she asked.

"No, but I can," Frances said.

"I think it would be wise," Gigi suggested.

"Frances, . . . I have shocking royal news: you are a
princess too!"

Frances thought she might faint, but the moment passed.

"How do you know?" she asked. "And why has my family been keeping this from me? Does this mean that my daddy is a king?"

This thought had never occurred to Gigi. Life was becoming very confusing. She was now surrounded by royalty.

That night she asked, "Daddy, are you a king?"

"Why would you think that?" he said.

"If I am a princess, you must be a king."

"Well, you are a daughter of a very great King," Daddy said. "He is King above any other king."

Big tears began to pool in the corners of Gigi's eyes. "Are you not my daddy?" she asked.

"Of course I am," Daddy said, squeezing her tightly. "But we are children of the greatest King of all. This King rules over everything there is, and you are His daughter. You are God's little princess! Now it's time to get to sleep. Goodnight, Gigi. Sweet dreams."

"Goodnight, Daddy."

Gigi snuggled into bed with her royal pink phone on the pillow beside her. "Just wait till I tell Frances my news tomorrow, Lord Fluffy! She's sure to faint this time.

I wonder," she said, patting her unruly hair, "just exactly when will I get my crown?"

The princess is
very beautiful. Her gown
is woven with gold. In her
beautiful clothes she is brought
to the king.

Psalm 45: 13-14